LET'S GET ALONG!

D0128367

It's Great to Work Together

Jordan Collins • Stuart Lynch

make believe ideas

"Good morning, class!" said Miss Clayton.

"I have **a surprise** for you!"

The children knew it must be something **exciting** because Miss Clayton couldn't stop smiling.

Sure enough, Miss Clayton announced that it was Treasure Hunt Day!

Teams would search the playground for objects.

The first team to find everything would win cool glow-in-the-dark markers!

"I'm going to split you into **teams**," Miss Clayton said.
"Then I'll give each team a set of **cards** showing objects,
such as a jump rope or a toy animal."

"You must **work together** to find all the objects and write down where they are."

Tia rushed out to the playground.

She was **more excited** about the game than anyone else in the class.

Her brother had brought home a set of markers last year
when his team had won.

She couldn't wait to have her own set!

Tia's teammates were Abby and Ryan.

They both looked at the cards . . . but Tia didn't.

"I bet together we can find everything really fast!" Abby said.

Tia **grabbed** the cards.

"My brother did the treasure hunt last year," Tia said.

"He told me where everything is."

"But Miss Clayton said we have to **work together!**" Ryan said.

"It will be **quicker** if you listen to me," said Tia. "You want to **win**, don't you?"

Tia began walking really fast. Ryan hurried after her.

"I can see a ball under the apple tree," he called out.

"One of the things we have to find is a ball."

Tia **ignored** him. The other groups were already

writing things down, and that made her walk even faster.

"There's a yo-yo near the hopscotch court," Abby said. "A yo-yo is on one of the cards."

"I told you," Tia said, "I already know where to find everything."

She couldn't understand why nobody was listening to her.

They were getting close to the field where
Tia's brother had found the objects last year.

Tia's heart was **beating fast.**

She couldn't wait to show her teammates that she'd been right all along.

When she got to the middle of the field, she looked around for the first time.
It was empty! Her heart sank.

"I . . . I . . . I . . . thought everything would be here," Tia said. "It was last year!"

In the distance, she heard Miss Clayton blow the whistle.
A team had **already won** the treasure hunt!

"We lost!" Tia said, looking shocked. "I can't believe it."

Ryan glared at Tia.
"I saw the ball,
but **you didn't listen**,"
he said.

"Yeah, and I saw the yo-yo,"
Abby added.

Tia suddenly **felt bad**
because she had
let her friends down.
Her stomach turned
into **knots**.

"I'm sorry," she said. "It's my fault that we've lost."

Abby took the cards from Tia.

"It's okay," she said, "but the next time you're on a team,

remember that it's important to **work together.**"

"And to **listen to each other,**" Ryan added.

"It's not nice to ignore people."

Tia realized she hadn't been **a good teammate.**
She **hadn't worked with her team,** or even **listened** to them.

"I'm really sorry," Tia said.

"If you'll be on my team again, I'll be a better teammate."

"Promise?" Ryan asked.

"Promise!" Tia said.

"I know," Tia added a moment later.

"Let's help clean up – as a team!"

"Good idea!" Abby said. "Let's go!"

"Here you go, Miss Clayton," Tia said.

"We've picked up everything for you."

"Wow! That's great," Miss Clayton said.

"What a **fantastic team!**"

Tia grinned. **Working together felt great!**

READING TOGETHER

The Let's Get Along! books have been written for parents, caregivers, and teachers to share with young children who are developing an awareness of their own behavior.

The books are intended to initiate thinking around behavior and empower children to create positive circumstances by managing their actions. Each book can be used to gently promote further discussion around the topic featured.

It's Great to Work Together is designed to help children realize that working as a team can lead to more positive results than ignoring other team members. Once you have read the story together, go back and talk about any similar experiences the children might have had with working well, or not working well, in groups. Ensure that children understand that almost everyone struggles with teamwork sometimes and that, like Tia, they can take steps to change their behavior and work better together.

As you read

By asking children questions as you read together, you can help them engage more deeply with the story. While it is important not to ask too many questions, you can try a few simple questions, such as:

- What do you think will happen next?
- Why do you think Tia did that?
- What would you do if you were Tia?
- How does Tia make up for not listening to the others?

Look at the pictures

Talk about the pictures. Are the characters smiling, laughing, frowning, or confused? Do their body positions show how they are feeling? Discuss why the characters might be responding this way. As children build their awareness of how others are reacting to them, they will find it easier to respond in an understanding way.

Questions you can ask after reading

To prompt further exploration of this behavior, you could ask children some of the following questions:

- Can you think of times when you work or play with others in a group or team?
- How do you feel when others take charge during group work or games?
- Can you think of any times when you haven't included everyone in the group? How do you think this made them feel? How might you do things differently next time?